This journal belongs to:

The Self-Exploration Journal

Disclaimer

This book is not intended to act as a substitute for medical advice or treatment. Any person with a condition requiring medical attention should consult a qualified medical practitioner or suitable therapist. The information provided in this book is stated to be truthful and consistent, in that any liability, in terms of inattention or otherwise, by any usage or abuse of any policies, processes, or directions contained within is the solitary and utter responsibility of the recipient reader. Under no circumstances will any legal responsibility or blame be held against the publisher for any reparation, damages, or monetary loss due to the information herein, either directly or indirectly.

The Self-Exploration Journal

One Year. A New Question Every Day

CREATED BY:

Zen Mirrors

How To Use This Journal

Every page of this book contains an inspiring quote and two days with different questions. There is enough space to answer the daily questions. If you need more space, you can use the blank pages at the end of this journal. We recommend setting a particular time each day for your journaling exercise. For example, during your morning routine or before you're going to bed. By choosing a particular time each day, you could integrate journaling as an empowering, simple and easy to follow habit in your life.

Throughout this book, you're going to find similar questions, mainly concerning the topics of gratefulness and your own strengths. We've done this to really bring these topics, which we often tend to forget, into the spotlight.

"It is never too late to be what you might have been."
George Eliot

Day 1 - Describe your inner dialogue when you want to take a risk.

Currently, I'm attempting to have a more positive inner dialogue. In the past my inner dialogue has been negative & discouraging. So now, even when considering taking a risk I'm still a little impulsive I'm having to learn to slow things down & think things through a little more.

Day 2 - What would be a completely different approach to improving your dating life?

Not blaming myself if things don't turn out. Stop saying yes to dates when I'm pretty sure that I'm not interested in the person. Stop trying to be so funny & have a regular conversation without feeling the need to be someone I'm not.

> **"Perhaps one did not want to be loved
> so much as to be understood."**
> George Orwell, *1984*

Day 3 - What is your favorite strategy for dealing with social anxiety?

_____
_____
_____
_____
_____
_____
_____
_____
_____
_____

Day 4 - In what way is your image different than your authentic self?

_____
_____
_____
_____
_____
_____
_____
_____
_____
_____
_____

"You will never be happy if you continue to search for what
happiness consists of. You will never live
if you are looking for the meaning of life."
Albert Camus

Day 5 - How much personal time do you actually need every
week, to function best?

_____

_____

_____

_____

_____

_____

_____

_____

Day 6 - If you should have a total makeover today, what would
you choose?

_____

_____

_____

_____

_____

_____

_____

_____

_____

"Be kind, for everyone you meet is fighting a harder battle."
Plato

Day 7 - Sit down for three minutes without doing anything. Set the alarm clock. Afterward, reflect on it. What happened?

_____

_____

_____

_____

_____

_____

_____

_____

_____

Day 8 - Which social conditions prevent you from living the life you want?

_____

_____

_____

_____

_____

_____

_____

_____

_____

_____

"Nobody has ever measured, not even poets,
how much the heart can hold."
Zelda Fitzgerald

Day 9 - Describe your comfort zone?

_____

_____

_____

_____

_____

_____

_____

_____

_____

Day 10 - What do you do for fun?

_____

_____

_____

_____

_____

_____

_____

_____

_____

_____

**"Nobody has ever measured, not even poets,
how much the heart can hold."**
Zelda Fitzgerald

Day 11 - If you go back in time, what was your favorite age or time growing up?

_____
_____
_____
_____
_____
_____
_____
_____
_____
_____
_____

Day 12 - What would surprise most people about you and why?

_____
_____
_____
_____
_____
_____
_____
_____
_____
_____
_____

"And those who were seen dancing were thought to be insane by those who could not hear the music."
Friedrich Nietzsche

Day 13 - How do you take care of your greatest strength?

_____

_____

_____

_____

_____

_____

_____

_____

_____

_____

Day 14 - When you are really under pressure, what do you need from your friends?

_____

_____

_____

_____

_____

_____

_____

_____

_____

_____

"Like all magnificent things, it's very simple."
Natalie Babbitt, *Tuck Everlasting*

Day 15 - If you would lose your income right now, how long could you live on your savings? How does the answer make you feel?

_____

_____

_____

_____

_____

_____

_____

_____

_____

Day 16 - How do you value your health?

_____

_____

_____

_____

_____

_____

_____

_____

_____

"Don't go around saying the world owes you a living. The world owes you nothing. It was here first."
Mark Twain

Day 17 - If you'd guess, how would your life look like in five years?

_____

_____

_____

_____

_____

_____

_____

_____

_____

_____

Day 18 - Describe the opposite of courage.

_____

_____

_____

_____

_____

_____

_____

_____

_____

_____

**"I like nonsense, it wakes up the brain cells.
Fantasy is a necessary ingredient in living."**
Dr. Seuss

Day 19 - Write down five past achievements you're proud of.

_____

_____

_____

_____

_____

_____

_____

_____

_____

_____

Day 20 - What is your mission in life?

_____

_____

_____

_____

_____

_____

_____

_____

_____

_____

_____

"I have not failed. I've just found 10,000 ways that won't work."
Thomas A. Edison

Day 21 - What are the pros of being insecure?

_____

_____

_____

_____

_____

_____

_____

_____

_____

Day 22 - Why do you feel the need to improve yourself?

_____

_____

_____

_____

_____

_____

_____

_____

_____

_____

"Your task is not to seek for love, but merely to seek and find all the barriers within yourself that you have built against it."
Rumi

Day 23 - What are five things you could do to improve your relationship with yourself?

Day 24 - What is your favorite strategy for pleasing others?

"The most courageous act is still to think for yourself. Aloud."
Coco Chanel

Day 25 – Do you consider naivety a strength or a weakness? Why?

_____

_____

_____

_____

_____

_____

_____

_____

_____

_____

Day 26 – What are you obsessed about and why?

_____

_____

_____

_____

_____

_____

_____

_____

_____

_____

_____

**"If you expect nothing from somebody
you are never disappointed."**
Sylvia Plath, *The Bell Jar*

Day 27 - In what ways did your parents shaped your
life positively?

_____
_____
_____
_____
_____
_____
_____
_____
_____

Day 28 - In what ways did your parents shaped your
life negatively?

_____
_____
_____
_____
_____
_____
_____
_____
_____

"Those who don't believe in magic will never find it."
Roald Dahl

Day 29 - What makes it difficult for you to embrace
the unknown?

Day 30 - Describe your ideal financial situation?

"There is nothing either good or bad, but thinking makes it so."
William Shakespeare, *Hamlet*

Day 31 - Are you a romantic? Why or why not?

_____

_____

_____

_____

_____

_____

_____

_____

_____

_____

_____

Day 32 - When was the last time you did something unusual?

_____

_____

_____

_____

_____

_____

_____

_____

_____

_____

_____

"Happiness is a warm puppy."
Charles M. Schulz

Day 33 - What is your biggest source of energy?

Day 34 - Could you handle more responsibility in your job?
Why or why not?

"What is a friend? A single soul dwelling in two bodies."
Aristotle

Day 35 - Do you feel love is overrated? Why or why not?

_____

_____

_____

_____

_____

_____

_____

_____

_____

_____

Day 36 - Write down three things you could do to improve your social life.

_____

_____

_____

_____

_____

_____

_____

_____

_____

_____

_____

"Love is so short, forgetting is so long."
Pablo Neruda, Love

Day 37 - Describe your three biggest fears.

_____
_____
_____
_____
_____
_____
_____
_____
_____
_____

Day 38 - Write down the names of all the people in your life who improve your overall well being.

_____
_____
_____
_____
_____
_____
_____
_____
_____
_____
_____

**"Only someone who is well prepared
has the opportunity to improvise."**
Ingmar Bergman

Day 39 - Do your negative thoughts serve any purpose?.

Day 40 - What characteristic would you like to have more of?

"Courage is the most important of all the virtues because without courage, you can't practice any other virtue consistently."
Maya Angelou

Day 41 - Write down three things you could do to better protect your time.

_____

_____

_____

_____

_____

_____

_____

_____

_____

_____

Day 42 - When do you often criticize yourself?

_____

_____

_____

_____

_____

_____

_____

_____

_____

_____

**"Never let your sense of morals
prevent you from doing what is right."**
Isaac Asimov, *Foundation*

Day 43 - Can people rely on you? Why or why not?

_____
_____
_____
_____
_____
_____
_____
_____
_____
_____

Day 44 - Are you a follower or a leader?

_____
_____
_____
_____
_____
_____
_____
_____
_____
_____

"You cannot protect yourself from sadness without protecting yourself from happiness."
Jonathan Safran Foer

Day 45 – How do you define your authentic self?

_____

_____

_____

_____

_____

_____

_____

_____

_____

_____

Day 46 – Write down three things that have a negative influence on your health.

_____

_____

_____

_____

_____

_____

_____

_____

_____

_____

"If you remember me, then I don't care if everyone else forgets."
Haruki Murakami, *Kafka on the Shore*

Day 47 - Write down three things that have a positive influence on your social life.

_____

_____

_____

_____

_____

_____

_____

_____

_____

_____

_____

Day 48 - Do you consider yourself a perfectionist?

_____

_____

_____

_____

_____

_____

_____

_____

_____

_____

_____

_____

"Every child is an artist.
The problem is how to remain an artist once he grows up."
Pablo Picasso

Day 49 - What one new skill would you like to learn in the next five years?

_____

_____

_____

_____

_____

_____

_____

_____

_____

_____

Day 50 - Is sarcasm one of your strengths or your weaknesses?

_____

_____

_____

_____

_____

_____

_____

_____

_____

_____

"The simple things are also the most extraordinary things, and only the wise can see them."
Paulo Coelho, *The Alchemist*

Day 51 - Can you easily forgive? Why or why not?

Day 52 - What three good deeds have you done for others in the last week?

"The future belongs to those who believe in the beauty of their dreams."
Eleanor Roosevelt

Day 53 - What is your favorite way to procrastinate?

_____
_____
_____
_____
_____
_____
_____
_____
_____
_____

Day 54 - Your favorite childhood memory.

_____
_____
_____
_____
_____
_____
_____
_____
_____
_____
_____

**"Sometimes you make choices in life
and sometimes choices make you."**
Gayle Forman, *If I Stay*

Day 55 - Are you really *living* your life?

Day 56 - To what kind of people are you attracted to?

"You cannot swim for new horizons until you have courage to lose sight of the shore."
William Faulkner

Day 57 – What kind of people are attracted to you?

_____
_____
_____
_____
_____
_____
_____
_____
_____
_____

Day 58 – What are your thoughts on fame?

_____
_____
_____
_____
_____
_____
_____
_____
_____
_____
_____

"Life's under no obligation to give us what we expect."
Margaret Mitchell

Day 59 - Describe the essentials of a good friendship.

Day 60 - Write down three things that give you a stressed feeling.

"If you love somebody, let them go, for if they return, they were always yours. If they don't, they never were."
Kahlil Gibran

Day 61 - How can you encourage yourself to take a step back in stressful situations?

_____
_____
_____
_____
_____
_____
_____
_____
_____

Day 62 - Is goal setting important to you? Why or why not?

_____
_____
_____
_____
_____
_____
_____
_____
_____
_____

"By three methods we may learn wisdom: First, by reflection, which is noblest; Second, by imitation, which is easiest; and third by experience, which is the bitterest."
Confucius

Day 63 - If you *had* to set three goals for the next three months, what would they be?

_____

_____

_____

_____

_____

_____

_____

_____

_____

Day 64 - Describe yourself in three words.

_____

_____

_____

_____

_____

_____

_____

_____

_____

"We do not need magic to transform our world. We carry all the power we need inside ourselves already."
J.K. Rowling

Day 65 - Describe your (ideal) love partner in five words.

Day 66 - What is your best health achievement so far?

"I have no special talents. I am only passionately curious."
Albert Einstein

Day 67 - Where do you often think about, before you go to bed?

_____

_____

_____

_____

_____

_____

_____

_____

_____

_____

Day 68 - How can you encourage yourself to do the things you want to do?

_____

_____

_____

_____

_____

_____

_____

_____

_____

_____

"None but ourselves can free our minds."
Bob Marley

Day 69 - What are the things you strongly dislike or hate?

_____

_____

_____

_____

_____

_____

_____

_____

_____

_____

Day 70 - Why do you feel the need to be with others?

_____

_____

_____

_____

_____

_____

_____

_____

_____

_____

**"People generally see what they look for,
and hear what they listen for."**
Harper Lee, *To Kill a Mockingbird*

Day 71 - Write down three things that you could do to feel
better about yourself.

_____

_____

_____

_____

_____

_____

_____

_____

_____

_____

Day 72 - How could you become a better listener?

_____

_____

_____

_____

_____

_____

_____

_____

_____

_____

"There is nothing in the world so irresistibly contagious as laughter and good humor."
Charles Dickens, *A Christmas Carol*

Day 73 - Write down three things that make you happy.

_____

_____

_____

_____

_____

_____

_____

_____

_____

_____

Day 74 - Can you actually handle more financial success?

_____

_____

_____

_____

_____

_____

_____

_____

_____

_____

"Life has no meaning. Each of us has meaning and we bring it to
life. It is a waste to be asking the question
when you are the answer."
Joseph Campbell

Day 75 - What beliefs did you 'borrow' from other people?

_____

_____

_____

_____

_____

_____

_____

_____

_____

_____

Day 76 - Do you feel you often have to explain your choices to
other people?

_____

_____

_____

_____

_____

_____

_____

_____

_____

"It is better to fail in originality than to succeed in imitation."
Herman Melville

Day 77 - How could you influence the foreseeable future for the better?

_____
_____
_____
_____
_____
_____
_____
_____
_____
_____
_____

Day 78 - What is your best characteristic and why?

_____
_____
_____
_____
_____
_____
_____
_____
_____
_____
_____

"If you look for **perfection**, you'll **never** be content."
Leo Tolstoy, *Anna Karenina*

Day 79 - How does your ideal love life look like?

_____

_____

_____

_____

_____

_____

_____

_____

_____

_____

Day 80 - What frequent lies have you told to protect
your image?

_____

_____

_____

_____

_____

_____

_____

_____

_____

"Trust yourself. You know more than you think you do."
Benjamin Spock

Day 81 - What kind of people make you feel uncomfortable?

_____

_____

_____

_____

_____

_____

_____

_____

_____

_____

Day 82 - What emotions are you suppressing and how does that makes you feel?

_____

_____

_____

_____

_____

_____

_____

_____

_____

_____

"The world as we have created it is a process of our thinking. It cannot be changed without changing our thinking."
Albert Einstein

Day 83 - How is the certainty of death influencing your life choices?

_____

_____

_____

_____

_____

_____

_____

_____

_____

_____

Day 84 - If you had a three month holiday one week from now, what would you do?

_____

_____

_____

_____

_____

_____

_____

_____

_____

_____

**"It is amazing how complete is the delusion
that beauty is goodness."**
Leo Tolstoy, *The Kreutzer Sonata*

Day 85 - What habit(s) has a negative influence on your life?

Day 86 - In what area of your life are you struggling and why?

"To be yourself in a world that is constantly trying to make you something else is the greatest accomplishment."
Ralph Waldo Emerson

Day 87 - What lesson(s) you had and/or have to learn the hard way?

_____
_____
_____
_____
_____
_____
_____
_____
_____
_____

Day 88 - How could you be more understanding to the people closest to you?

_____
_____
_____
_____
_____
_____
_____
_____
_____
_____

"Never be afraid to sit awhile and think."
Lorraine Hansberry

Day 89 - Describe your perfect date night.

_____
_____
_____
_____
_____
_____
_____
_____
_____
_____

Day 90 - What is your destiny on this planet?

_____
_____
_____
_____
_____
_____
_____
_____
_____
_____

"Adventure is worthwhile in itself."
Amelia Earhart

Day 91 - Write down five things you could do to relax.

Day 92 - How do you define the difference between good and evil?

"Our imagination flies -- we are its shadow on the earth."
Vladimir Nabokov

Day 93 - What is your definition of love?

_____

_____

_____

_____

_____

_____

_____

_____

_____

_____

Day 94 - Do you feel younger or older than your actual age?
Why?

_____

_____

_____

_____

_____

_____

_____

_____

_____

_____

_____

"Romance is the glamour which turns the dust of everyday life into a golden haze. "
Elinor Glyn

Day 95 - What three things make you stand out from other people?

_____

_____

_____

_____

_____

_____

_____

_____

_____

_____

Day 96 - What three questions would you ask a financial advisor?

_____

_____

_____

_____

_____

_____

_____

_____

_____

_____

"Child, child, do you not see? For each of us comes a time when we must be more than what we are."
Lloyd Alexander, The Black Cauldron

Day 97 - What is the most courageous thing you've ever done in your life?

_____

_____

_____

_____

_____

_____

_____

_____

_____

Day 98 - Sit down for five minutes without doing anything. Set the alarm clock. Afterward reflect on it. What happened?

_____

_____

_____

_____

_____

_____

_____

_____

_____

"That was one of the virtues of being a pessimist: nothing was ever as bad as you thought it would be."
James Jones, *From Here to Eternity*

Day 99 - Which social conditions are actually improving your life?

Day 100 - What does your body say no to?

"I am a part of all that I have met."
Alfred Tennyson, *The Complete Poetical Works of Tennyson*

Day 101 - Do you often identify yourself with what you're having (such as friendships, appearances, possessions)?

Day 102 - What about the media annoys you most?

**"The present changes the past.
Looking back you do not find what you left behind."**
Kiran Desai, *The Inheritance of Loss*

Day 103 - Describe what is just out of reach of your comfort
zone right now.

_____

_____

_____

_____

_____

_____

_____

_____

_____

_____

Day 104 - Do you feel sexually satisfied? Why or why not?

_____

_____

_____

_____

_____

_____

_____

_____

_____

_____

"Autumn is a second spring when every leaf is a flower."
Albert Camus

Day 105 – What is for you the best way to heal when you feel sick?

_____

_____

_____

_____

_____

_____

_____

_____

_____

_____

Day 106 – Describe your favorite night out with friends.

_____

_____

_____

_____

_____

_____

_____

_____

_____

**"Peace cannot be kept by force;
it can only be achieved by understanding."**
Albert Einstein

Day 107 - Are you an introvert or an extrovert and why?

_____

_____

_____

_____

_____

_____

_____

_____

_____

_____

Day 108 - Do you feel comfortable in your own skin?
Why or why not?

_____

_____

_____

_____

_____

_____

_____

_____

_____

_____

"I bet you could sometimes find all the mysteries of the universe in someone's hand."
Benjamin Alire Sáenz, *Aristotle and Dante Discover the Secrets of the Universe*

Day 109 – Is their still *music* left in you?

Day 110 – Write down at least three reasons why you worry what other people think of you.

"One of the deep secrets of life is that all that is really worth the doing is what we do for others."
Lewis Carroll

Day 111 - Why could you be optimistic about humanity?

_____
_____
_____
_____
_____
_____
_____
_____
_____
_____

Day 112 - What are your thoughts on charity?

_____
_____
_____
_____
_____
_____
_____
_____
_____
_____

**"He who knows all the answers
has not been asked all the questions."**
Confucius

Day 113 - How could you integrate more joyful moments in your life? Pick one of these answers and make a commitment with yourself to integrate it in your life this week.

_____

_____

_____

_____

_____

_____

_____

_____

Day 114 - What is your greatest weakness? And how do you deal with it?

_____

_____

_____

_____

_____

_____

_____

_____

_____

_____

**"I am not interested in being original.
I am interested in being true."**
Agostinho da Silva

Day 115 - What about social conditions annoys you most?

Day 116 - What is your best financial achievement so far?

"I don't think there is any truth. There are only points of view. "
Allen Ginsberg

Day 117 - What makes it difficult for you to get out of your comfort zone?

_____

_____

_____

_____

_____

_____

_____

_____

_____

_____

Day 118 - What are the pros of being imperfect?

_____

_____

_____

_____

_____

_____

_____

_____

_____

_____

_____

"You get what anybody gets - you get a lifetime."
Neil Gaiman, *Preludes & Nocturnes*

Day 119 - What one small step could you take this week to improve your self-confidence?

Day 120 - Who are your role models?

"Let us be grateful to the people who make us happy; they are the charming gardeners who make our souls blossom."
Marcel Proust

Day 121 - What kind of secret feelings do you have?

_____
_____
_____
_____
_____
_____
_____
_____
_____
_____

Day 122 - Write down three things that have a positive influence on your love life.

_____
_____
_____
_____
_____
_____
_____
_____
_____
_____

"I've begun to realize that you can listen to silence and learn from it. It has a quality and a dimension all its own."
Chaim Potok, *The Chosen*

Day 123 - If you could solve one problem in your life right now, what would it be?

_____

_____

_____

_____

_____

_____

_____

_____

_____

Day 124 - Is loyalty one of your strengths or your weaknesses?

_____

_____

_____

_____

_____

_____

_____

_____

_____

"Nobody can hurt me without my permission."
Mahatma Gandhi

Day 125 - If you could solve one problem in your life right now, what would it be?

_____

_____

_____

_____

_____

_____

_____

_____

_____

Day 126 - Do you attract the love partner(s) you want?

_____

_____

_____

_____

_____

_____

_____

_____

_____

_____

"Those who cannot change their minds cannot change anything."
George Bernard Shaw

Day 127 - Describe your relationship with yourself.

_____

_____

_____

_____

_____

_____

_____

_____

_____

_____

Day 128 - Are you easily influenced by the news?

_____

_____

_____

_____

_____

_____

_____

_____

_____

_____

_____

**"Never attempt to teach a pig to sing;
it wastes your time and annoys the pig."**
Robert Heinlein, *Time Enough for Love*

Day 129 - What do you most often do, when you're
feeling lonely?

_____

_____

_____

_____

_____

_____

_____

_____

_____

_____

Day 130 - What one small step could you take this week to
improve your health?

_____

_____

_____

_____

_____

_____

_____

_____

_____

_____

**"Educating the mind without educating the heart
is no education at all."**
Aristotle

Day 131 - What could you learn from your role models?

Day 132 - What part(s) of yourself do you find difficult
to accept?

**"Man only likes to count his troubles;
he doesn't calculate his happiness."**
Fyodor Dostoevsky, *Notes from Underground*

Day 133 - Describe the opposite of happiness.

Day 134 - What three good deeds people have done for you in
the last week?

"Don't cry because it's over, smile because it happened."
Dr. Seuss

Day 135 - Who would you like to be with now and why?

_____

_____

_____

_____

_____

_____

_____

_____

_____

_____

Day 137 - What three good deeds did you do last week?

_____

_____

_____

_____

_____

_____

_____

_____

_____

_____

"Every saint has a past, and every sinner has a future."
Oscar Wilde

Day 137 – What is your favorite strategy to avoid/deal
with conflicts?

Day 138 – Write down three things that have a positive
influence on your financial situation.

"No one ever told me that grief felt so like fear."
C.S. Lewis, *A Grief Observed*

Day 139 - In what situations do you often feel the trigger to abandon your authentic self?

Day 140 - Why is it attractive to have you as a love partner?

"Most men would rather deny a hard truth than face it."
George R.R. Martin, *A Game of Thrones*

Day 141 - Do you often analyze what other people might think of you? Why or why not?

Day 142 - What three choices you've made in the past has shaped your destiny?

"Blessed are the hearts that can bend; they shall never be broken."
Albert Camus

Day 143 - Write down three things that have a negative influence on your self-confidence.

_____
_____
_____
_____
_____
_____
_____
_____
_____
_____

Day 144 - What are your thoughts on male / female roles?

_____
_____
_____
_____
_____
_____
_____
_____
_____
_____
_____

**"We'd get sick on too many cookies,
but ever so much sicker on no cookies at all."**
Sinclair Lewis

Day 145 - If you could only ask three questions on the first date night, what would these questions be?

_____

_____

_____

_____

_____

_____

_____

_____

_____

Day 146 - Write down one nice thing you could do for someone else today. Afterward, reflect on this page how it felt.

_____

_____

_____

_____

_____

_____

_____

_____

_____

_____

"One must dare to be happy."
Gertrude Stein

Day 147 - Write down seven of your most important values.

Day 148 - What are your thoughts on an afterlife?

"Name the greatest of all inventors. Accident."
Mark Twain

Day 149 – How do you contemplate important decisions?

Day 150 – Write down a completely different approach then you would normally do, to come to an important decision.

"I must learn to be content with being happier than I deserve."
Jane Austen, *Pride and Prejudice*

Day 151 - Do you find life demanding? Why or why not?

_____

_____

_____

_____

_____

_____

_____

_____

_____

_____

Day 152 - What makes you feel offended and why?

_____

_____

_____

_____

_____

_____

_____

_____

_____

_____

"The finest of pleasures are always the unexpected ones."
Erin Morgenstern, *The Night Circus*

Day 153 - What would be a completely different approach to dealing with rejection?

Day 154 - What five things make you feel grateful for your personal relationships?

"The most certain sign of wisdom is cheerfulness."
Michel de Montaigne

Day 155 - What are your limiting beliefs?

Day 156 - Look at your list of yesterday. Which of these beliefs are false and why?

"All happiness depends on courage and work."
Honoré de Balzac

Day 157 – What are the three questions you would ask your future 75-year old self?

_____

_____

_____

_____

_____

_____

_____

_____

_____

_____

Day 158 – What kind of people are often ask for your help?

_____

_____

_____

_____

_____

_____

_____

_____

_____

_____

"It is more fun to talk with someone who doesn't use long, difficult words but rather short, easy words like "What about lunch?"
A. A. Milne, *Winnie-the-Pooh*

Day 159 - What kind of conversations do you have with the five people closest to you?

_____

_____

_____

_____

_____

_____

_____

_____

_____

Day 160 - How do you deal with people trying to come close to you?

_____

_____

_____

_____

_____

_____

_____

_____

_____

"I am beginning to learn that it is the sweet, simple things of life which are the real ones after all."
Laura Ingalls Wilder

Day 161 - Who is in need of your voice?

Day 162 - What are the gifts you deliver to this world?

"Whenever you feel like criticizing anyone...just remember that all the people in this world haven't had the advantages that you've had."
F. Scott Fitzgerald, *The Great Gatsby*

Day 163 - When do you feel the most like yourself?

Day 164 - What would be a completely different approach to dealing with risks?

"That which you believe becomes your world."
Richard Matheson, *What Dreams May Come*

Day 165 – What does self-confidence means to you?

_____

_____

_____

_____

_____

_____

_____

_____

_____

_____

Day 166 – What five things make you feel grateful for your personal health?

_____

_____

_____

_____

_____

_____

_____

_____

_____

"When you are content to be simply yourself and don't compare or compete, everyone will respect you."
Lao Tzu, *Tao Te Ching*

Day 167 - What matters most to you in personal relationships?

Day 168 - Do you dare to publicly commit to your goals? Why or why not?

"There are only two ways to live your life. One is as though nothing is a miracle. The other is as though everything is a miracle."
Albert Einstein

Day 169 - What scares you most when you think about death?

_____
_____
_____
_____
_____
_____
_____
_____
_____

Day 170 - Do you dare to publicly commit to your goals?
Why or why not?

_____
_____
_____
_____
_____
_____
_____
_____
_____
_____

"I don't think of all the misery, but of the beauty that still remains."
Anne Frank, *The Diary of a Young Girl*

Day 171 - What would be a completely different approach to take care of your health?

_____

_____

_____

_____

_____

_____

_____

_____

_____

_____

Day 172 - Describe your inner dialogue when you want to approach a stranger.

_____

_____

_____

_____

_____

_____

_____

_____

_____

_____

"You'll miss the best things if you keep your eyes shut."
Dr. Seuss, *I Can Read With My Eyes Shut!*

Day 173 - What five things make you feel grateful about
self-development?

_____

_____

_____

_____

_____

_____

_____

_____

_____

Day 174 - What could be a strategy to accept yourself
no matter what?

_____

_____

_____

_____

_____

_____

_____

_____

_____

_____

"No winter lasts forever; no spring skips its turn."
Hal Borland

Day 175 - What is the one advice you would give yourself 1 year in the future?

_____

_____

_____

_____

_____

_____

_____

_____

_____

_____

Day 176 - What five things make you feel grateful for your job?

_____

_____

_____

_____

_____

_____

_____

_____

_____

_____

_____

**"There's nowhere you can be
that isn't where you're meant to be..."**
John Lennon

Day 177 - What could be a strategy to be more loving and kind
to the people around you?

_____

_____

_____

_____

_____

_____

_____

_____

_____

Day 178 - What were the three favorite things you did as a kid?

_____

_____

_____

_____

_____

_____

_____

_____

_____

"If you tell the truth, you don't have to remember anything."
Mark Twain

Day 179 - What are three problems you would like to solve in your life?

_____

_____

_____

_____

_____

_____

_____

_____

_____

_____

Day 180 - What are your thoughts on depression?

_____

_____

_____

_____

_____

_____

_____

_____

_____

_____

"My religion is very simple. My religion is kindness."
Dalai Lama XIV

Day 181 - What prevents you from living to your true potential?

_____

_____

_____

_____

_____

_____

_____

_____

_____

Day 182 - If you looked back on the past few months, how did you grow personally?

_____

_____

_____

_____

_____

_____

_____

_____

_____

_____

"Man, when you lose your laugh you lose your footing."
Ken Kesey, *One Flew Over the Cuckoo's Nest*

Day 185 - What past experiences have most shaped your spiritual life?

_____
_____
_____
_____
_____
_____
_____
_____
_____
_____

Day 186 - If you could only ask three questions during a job interview for a new co-worker, what would these questions be?

_____
_____
_____
_____
_____
_____
_____
_____
_____
_____

"The way to get started is to quit talking and begin doing."
Walt Disney

Day 187 - Write down the three key things to maintain balance in your life.

_____

_____

_____

_____

_____

_____

_____

_____

_____

_____

Day 188 - What are your three favorite movies and why?

_____

_____

_____

_____

_____

_____

_____

_____

_____

_____

_____

"Respect other people's feelings. It might mean nothing to you,
but it could mean everything to them."
Roy T. Bennett

Day 189 - What is fake about how you portray
yourself to the world?

_____
_____
_____
_____
_____
_____
_____
_____
_____

Day 190 - How would you encourage someone else to follow
their dreams?

_____
_____
_____
_____
_____
_____
_____
_____
_____
_____

"Music is ... A higher revelation than all Wisdom & Philosophy"
Ludwig van Beethoven

Day 191 - How would your (ideal) love partner describe you to other people?

_____

_____

_____

_____

_____

_____

_____

_____

_____

_____

Day 192 - How would you encourage someone else to follow their dreams?

_____

_____

_____

_____

_____

_____

_____

_____

_____

_____

"Do no harm and leave the world a better place than you found it."
Patricia Cornwell

Day 193 - What is more or less your net worth? (Net worth is what you own (possession, savings, investing, real estate, etc.), minus what you owe (loans, mortgage, etc.)

Day 194 - What are your three favorite songs and why?

"Words were different when they lived inside of you."
Benjamin Alire Sáenz, *Aristotle and Dante Discover the
Secrets of the Universe*

Day 195 – If you could only ask three questions to your role
model, what would these questions be?

_____
_____
_____
_____
_____
_____
_____
_____
_____
_____

Day 196 – Describe the opposite of love.

_____
_____
_____
_____
_____
_____
_____
_____
_____
_____
_____
_____

"To love another person is to see the face of God."
Victor Hugo, *Les Misérables*

Day 197 - How would you describe your most courageous and self-confident self?

Day 198 - Do you easily trust others? Why or why not?

**"The happiness of your life
depends upon the quality of your thoughts."**
Marcus Aurelius, *Meditations*

Day 199 - What do you actually need to survive?

_____

_____

_____

_____

_____

_____

_____

_____

_____

Day 200 - What is your favorite strategy to deal with rejection?

_____

_____

_____

_____

_____

_____

_____

_____

_____

_____

"Love makes your soul crawl out from its hiding place."
Zora Neale Hurston

Day 201 - Write down five things that have a positive influence on your self-confidence.

_____

_____

_____

_____

_____

_____

_____

_____

_____

_____

Day 202 - Write down three things that make you feel incredibly grateful.

_____

_____

_____

_____

_____

_____

_____

_____

_____

_____

"I am not afraid of storms, for I am learning how to sail my ship."
Louisa May Alcott, *Little Women*

Day 203 - What sexual fantasies are you suppressing and how does that makes you feel?

_____

_____

_____

_____

_____

_____

_____

_____

_____

Day 204 - If death is certain, do you really *live* your life?

_____

_____

_____

_____

_____

_____

_____

_____

_____

"What draws people to be friends is that they see the same truth. They share it."
C. S. Lewis

Day 205 - The three best things that happened last month.

_____
_____
_____
_____
_____
_____
_____
_____
_____

Day 206 - What does weather do to your overall mood?

_____
_____
_____
_____
_____
_____
_____
_____
_____
_____

"The earth laughs in flowers."
Ralph Waldo Emerson

Day 207 – What strong political opinions do you have?

Day 208 – When do you feel the need to isolate yourself?

"The things you used to own, now they own you."
Chuck Palahniuk, *Fight Club*

Day 209 - What is your definition of comfort?

_____
_____
_____
_____
_____
_____
_____
_____
_____
_____

Day 210 - How would you describe your most fearful self?

_____
_____
_____
_____
_____
_____
_____
_____
_____
_____
_____

"The real voyage of discovery consists not in seeking new landscapes, but in having new eyes."
Marcel Proust

Day 211 - What three small actions could you take to improve your willpower?

_____

_____

_____

_____

_____

_____

_____

_____

_____

_____

Day 212 - Write down one nice thing you could do for yourself today. Afterward, reflect on this page how it felt.

_____

_____

_____

_____

_____

_____

_____

_____

_____

"Your silence will not protect you."
Audre Lorde, *Sister Outsider: Essays and Speeches*

Day 213 – What are the three things that drive you the most?

_____

_____

_____

_____

_____

_____

_____

_____

_____

_____

Day 214 – What would be a completely different approach to handle your financial situation?

_____

_____

_____

_____

_____

_____

_____

_____

_____

_____

"Life is a mirror: if you frown at it, it frowns back; if you smile, it returns the greeting."
William Makepeace Thackeray

Day 215 – Do you believe *success* is a choice? Why or why not?

_____

_____

_____

_____

_____

_____

_____

_____

_____

_____

Day 216 – How does the previous question made you feel when you read it?

_____

_____

_____

_____

_____

_____

_____

_____

_____

_____

"When you read a book, you hold another's mind in your hands."
James Burke

Day 217 - Sit down for ten minutes without doing anything. Set the alarm clock. Afterward, reflect on it. What happened?

_____

_____

_____

_____

_____

_____

_____

_____

_____

Day 218 - Do you often identify yourself with what you're doing (such as your creative enterprises, personal development, your job or own business)?

_____

_____

_____

_____

_____

_____

_____

_____

_____

"Be glad. Be good. Be brave."
Eleanor Hodgman Porter

Day 219 - Write down three major turning points in your life.

_____
_____
_____
_____
_____
_____
_____
_____
_____
_____

Day 220 - What is your favorite strategy to deal with uncomfortable conversations?

_____
_____
_____
_____
_____
_____
_____
_____
_____
_____
_____

**"At the end of the day,
we can endure much more than we think we can."**
Frida Kahlo

Day 221 - What would you like to do, that you're actually not allowed to do?

_____

_____

_____

_____

_____

_____

_____

_____

_____

_____

Day 222 - What are three small actions you could take to improve your intelligence?

_____

_____

_____

_____

_____

_____

_____

_____

_____

_____

"A person often meets his destiny on the road he took to avoid it."
Jean de La Fontaine, Fables

Day 223 - How easily are you influenced by others?

_____

_____

_____

_____

_____

_____

_____

_____

_____

_____

Day 224 - What one small step could you take this week to improve your financial situation?

_____

_____

_____

_____

_____

_____

_____

_____

_____

_____

"Ever has it been that love knows not its own depth
until the hour of separation."
Kahlil Gibran

Day 225 - What are your thoughts on feminism?

_____

_____

_____

_____

_____

_____

_____

_____

_____

_____

Day 226 - Describe your inner dialogue when you enter a new
environment (such as a nightclub, network event, new job).

_____

_____

_____

_____

_____

_____

_____

_____

_____

_____

"Between two evils, I always pick the one I never tried before."
Mae West

Day 227 - How could you change someone else's life for the better today?

_____

_____

_____

_____

_____

_____

_____

_____

_____

Day 228 - Who do you want to be one year from now? Describe in as much detail as you could.

_____

_____

_____

_____

_____

_____

_____

_____

_____

_____

"I've lived through some terrible things in my life, some of which actually happened."
Mark Twain

Day 229 - What is one good habit you want to cultivate in the next coming months?

_____

_____

_____

_____

_____

_____

_____

_____

_____

Day 230 - Describe your inner dialogue when you do something, you know is not right.

_____

_____

_____

_____

_____

_____

_____

_____

_____

_____

"The earth has its music for those who will listen"
Reginald Vincent Holmes, *Fireside Fancies*

Day 231 - What is the purpose behind your three most
important goals in life?

_____

_____

_____

_____

_____

_____

_____

_____

_____

Day 232 - In what way are you more privileged than others?

_____

_____

_____

_____

_____

_____

_____

_____

_____

_____

"Let the rain kiss you. Let the rain beat upon your head with silver liquid drops. Let the rain sing you a lullaby."
Langston Hughes

Day 233 - How would you call the period of your life right now?

_____

_____

_____

_____

_____

_____

_____

_____

_____

Day 234 - What are your thoughts on prayer?

_____

_____

_____

_____

_____

_____

_____

_____

_____

_____

"Even strength must bow to wisdom sometimes."
Rick Riordan, *The Lightning Thief*

Day 235 - Write down three things that have a negative influence on your love life.

_____

_____

_____

_____

_____

_____

_____

_____

_____

_____

Day 236 - What kind of image do you project to the world?

_____

_____

_____

_____

_____

_____

_____

_____

_____

_____

_____

**"The world is full of magic things,
patiently waiting for our senses to grow sharper."**
W.B. Yeats

Day 237 - Write down five things that make your life more than worthwhile.

_____

_____

_____

_____

_____

_____

_____

_____

_____

_____

Day 238 - What is your view on spirituality?

_____

_____

_____

_____

_____

_____

_____

_____

_____

_____

"Kind words can be short and easy to speak,
but their echoes are truly endless."
Mother Teresa

Day 239 - What task you should do, are you delaying for quite some time now?

_____

Day 240 - What friends or family members frequently have a negative influence on how you feel?

_____

**"That's what careless words do.
They make people love you a little less."**
Arundhati Roy, *The God of Small Things*

Day 241 - What is one of your weaknesses you could actually
consider as a blessing?

_____

_____

_____

_____

_____

_____

_____

_____

_____

_____

Day 242 - Write down three things that have a positive
influence on your health.

_____

_____

_____

_____

_____

_____

_____

_____

_____

_____

"The greatest enemy of knowledge is not ignorance,
it is the illusion of knowledge."
Daniel J. Boorstin

Day 243 - What are you living for?

_____

_____

_____

_____

_____

_____

_____

_____

_____

_____

Day 244 - Write down three things that have a bad influence on
your financial situation.

_____

_____

_____

_____

_____

_____

_____

_____

_____

_____

"Very few of us are what we seem."
Agatha Christie, The Man in the Mist

Day 245 - Are you treating yourself with the love and respect
you deserve?

_____

_____

_____

_____

_____

_____

_____

_____

_____

_____

Day 246 - What is your light in the darkness?

_____

_____

_____

_____

_____

_____

_____

_____

_____

_____

_____

"It is never too late to be wise."
Daniel Defoe, *Robinson Crusoe*

Day 247 - What would you do if you had no friends and family?

_____

_____

_____

_____

_____

_____

_____

_____

_____

_____

_____

_____

Day 248 - How could you show more of your true self?

_____

_____

_____

_____

_____

_____

_____

_____

_____

_____

_____

_____

"Time is the longest distance between two places."
Tennessee Williams, *The Glass Menagerie*

Day 249 - Describe how you would like to feel more often.

Day 250 - Pause for a minute. What have you been avoiding?

**"The only real prison is fear,
and the only real freedom is freedom from fear"**
Aung San Suu Kyi

Day 251 - Who are you willing to struggle for?

Day 252 - Do you allow yourself to feel your emotions?

"When one tugs at a single thing in nature, he finds it attached to
the rest of the world."
John Muir

Day 253 – Write down three things that have a negative
influence on your social life.

_____

_____

_____

_____

_____

_____

_____

_____

_____

_____

Day 254 – In what area of your life are you focusing too much
on the outcome.

_____

_____

_____

_____

_____

_____

_____

_____

_____

_____

"Hope is a waking dream."
Aristotle

Day 255 – What conversation do you need to have?

_____
_____
_____
_____
_____
_____
_____
_____
_____
_____

Day 256- Why are you committed to self-development?

_____
_____
_____
_____
_____
_____
_____
_____
_____
_____

"Happiness is something that comes into our lives through doors we don't even remember leaving open."
Rose Wilder Lane

Day 257 - Are your actions this month guided by love or fear?

_____
_____
_____
_____
_____
_____
_____
_____
_____
_____

Day 258 - In what area of your life have you been settling? Is it out of fear to lose comfort?

_____
_____
_____
_____
_____
_____
_____
_____
_____
_____

"There are two means of refuge from the misery of life — music and cats."
Albert Schweitzer

Day 259 - What past situation triggers you to self-pity?

_____

_____

_____

_____

_____

_____

_____

_____

_____

_____

Day 260 - How does your past hinders your ability to move forward?

_____

_____

_____

_____

_____

_____

_____

_____

_____

_____

"The beginning of love is the will to let those we love be perfectly themselves, the resolution not to twist them to fit our own image."
Thomas Merton, *The Way of Chuang Tzu*

Day 261 - What emotion do you need to give more space?

_____

_____

_____

_____

_____

_____

_____

_____

_____

_____

Day 262 - Write down your most difficult choice right now. What does your heart tells you to do?

_____

_____

_____

_____

_____

_____

_____

_____

_____

_____

"If there's a single lesson that life teaches us, it's that wishing doesn't make it so."
Lev Grossman, *The Magicians*

Day 263 - Do you feel confident enough to reveal your flaws? Why or why not?

_____

_____

_____

_____

_____

_____

_____

_____

_____

_____

Day 264 - In what area of your life do you feel most *alive*?

_____

_____

_____

_____

_____

_____

_____

_____

_____

_____

"Wheresoever you go, go with all your heart."
Confucius

Day 265 – How could being unapologetic help you to be more authentic?

Day 266 – What desire(s) did you give up to please others?

**"You can cut all the flowers
but you cannot keep Spring from coming."**
Pablo Neruda

Day 267 – What plan or goal actually no longer fits in your life?

_____

_____

_____

_____

_____

_____

_____

_____

_____

_____

Day 268 – What past situation triggers you to a feeling
of inadequacy?

_____

_____

_____

_____

_____

_____

_____

_____

_____

_____

"People demand freedom of speech as a compensation for the freedom of thought which they seldom use."
Søren Kierkegaard

Day 269 - What have you given up on, that still wants to be pursued?

_____

_____

_____

_____

_____

_____

_____

_____

_____

Day 270 - Choose one insecurity that you will help, accept and love today.

_____

_____

_____

_____

_____

_____

_____

_____

_____

"Don't bend; don't water it down; don't try to make it logical; don't edit your own soul according to the fashion. Rather, follow your most intense obsessions mercilessly."
Franz Kafka

Day 271 - How do you measure your success?

_____
_____
_____
_____
_____
_____
_____
_____
_____
_____
_____

Day 272 - How do you measure the success of others?

_____
_____
_____
_____
_____
_____
_____
_____
_____
_____
_____

"We've got to live, no matter how many skies have fallen."
D.H. Lawrence, *Lady Chatterley's Lover*

Day 273 – What is the silver lining of your current life situation?

_____

_____

_____

_____

_____

_____

_____

_____

_____

Day 274 – In what area of your life do you feel the need to take action and why?

_____

_____

_____

_____

_____

_____

_____

_____

_____

"So many things become beautiful when you really look."
Lauren Oliver, *Before I Fall*

Day 275 - What barriers do you keep creating, that hinders your success and happiness?

_____

_____

_____

_____

_____

_____

_____

_____

Day 276 - Sit down for twelve minutes without doing anything. Set the alarm clock. Afterward, reflect on it. What happened?

_____

_____

_____

_____

_____

_____

_____

_____

"What is that you express in your eyes?
It seems to me more than all the print I have read in my life."
Walt Whitman

Day 277 - Choose one painful memory that you will care for,
accept and give love to today..

Day 278 - What is your favorite strategy for dealing with chaos
in your life?

"If you ever find yourself in the wrong story, leave."
Mo Willems, *Goldilocks and the Three Dinosaurs*

Day 279 - Track what your spend for one week in an excel sheet, or on the blank pages at the end of this journal. Make three columns: What (groceries, sports membership, Starbucks coffee, night out with friends, etc.) – How much (money you spend) When (the date). Come back at the end of this week to this page and reflect on your spending habit. Questions you could ask, are: What surprises me the most? If I could do one thing differently next week, what would it be? How could I spend more money on experiences?

Day 280 - What makes you angry?

**"We are only as strong as we are united,
as weak as we are divided."**
J.K. Rowling, *Harry Potter and the Goblet of Fire*

Day 281 - What do you feel when you're connected with others?

_____

_____

_____

_____

_____

_____

_____

_____

_____

_____

Day 282 - What gave you hope in the last few weeks?

_____

_____

_____

_____

_____

_____

_____

_____

_____

_____

_____

"Most people are other people. Their thoughts are someone else's opinions, their lives a mimicry, their passions a quotation."
Oscar Wilde

Day 283 - Write down three compliments you received in the past few months.

_____

_____

_____

_____

_____

_____

_____

_____

_____

_____

Day 284 - What is the influence of self-denial in your life?

_____

_____

_____

_____

_____

_____

_____

_____

_____

"What lies behind us and what lies before us are tiny matters
compared to what lies within us."
Ralph Waldo Emerson

Day 285 - Write down one small victory you had this month.

_____

_____

_____

_____

_____

_____

_____

_____

_____

_____

Day 286 - What is your biggest challenge when it comes to
loving another person?

_____

_____

_____

_____

_____

_____

_____

_____

_____

_____

_____

**"Tell me, what is it you plan
to do with your one wild and precious life?"**
Mary Oliver

Day 287 - Do you take care of your body as if it is your temple?

_____

_____

_____

_____

_____

_____

_____

_____

_____

Day 288 - How could you improve your self-confidence when it
comes to your sexual life?

_____

_____

_____

_____

_____

_____

_____

_____

_____

"Enjoy it. Because it's happening."
Stephen Chbosky, *The Perks of Being a Wallflower*

Day 289 - How do you feel when you're the center of attention?

_____

_____

_____

_____

_____

_____

_____

_____

_____

_____

Day 290 - What three questions would you ask a psychologist?

_____

_____

_____

_____

_____

_____

_____

_____

_____

_____

_____

"Clouds come floating into my life, no longer to carry rain or usher storm, but to add color to my sunset sky."
Rabindranath Tagore, *Stray Birds*

Day 291 - What is your biggest challenge when it comes to feeling gratitude?

_____
_____
_____
_____
_____
_____
_____
_____
_____
_____

Day 292 - Do you often fear for the worst? Why or why not?

_____
_____
_____
_____
_____
_____
_____
_____
_____
_____

"Clouds come floating into my life, no longer to carry rain or usher storm, but to add color to my sunset sky."
Rabindranath Tagore, *Stray Birds*

Day 293 – Do you easily feel other people's emotions?

_____

_____

_____

_____

_____

_____

_____

_____

_____

_____

Day 294 – What are three small actions you could take to improve your memory?

_____

_____

_____

_____

_____

_____

_____

_____

_____

_____

"Without deviation from the norm, progress is not possible."
Frank Zappa

Day 295 - What are your thoughts on *being busy*?

Day 296 - What could you learn from your 18-year old self?

**"Success is getting what you want,
happiness is wanting what you get"**
W. P. Kinsella

Day 297 - Write down three insights you gained this week.

_____

_____

_____

_____

_____

_____

_____

_____

_____

_____

Day 298 - Do you believe vulnerability is a strength or a
weakness? Why?

_____

_____

_____

_____

_____

_____

_____

_____

_____

_____

**"Nothing is so painful to the human mind
as a great and sudden change."**
Mary Wollstonecraft Shelley, *Frankenstein*

Day 299 - How do you feel about following the rules?

Day 300 - In what area of your life do you find it difficult
to progress?

"I was within and without, simultaneously enchanted and repelled by the inexhaustible variety of life."
Fitzgerald F. Scott, *The Great Gatsby*

Day 301 - Do you believe having a vivid imagination is a strength or a weakness? Why?

_____

_____

_____

_____

_____

_____

_____

_____

_____

Day 302 - Name three meetings with a stranger that have shaped you positively.

_____

_____

_____

_____

_____

_____

_____

_____

_____

**"I was smiling yesterday, I am smiling today and I will smile
tomorrow. Simply because life is too short to cry for anything."**
Santosh Kalwar, *Quote Me Everyday*

Day 303 - Write down three things that could bring more
structure in your life?

Day 304 - Do you often sell yourself short? Why or why not?

**"You are imperfect, permanently and inevitably flawed.
And you are beautiful."**
Amy Bloom

Day 305 - How do you see your life five years from now?

_____

_____

_____

_____

_____

_____

_____

_____

_____

_____

Day 306 - What are your thoughts on traveling?

_____

_____

_____

_____

_____

_____

_____

_____

_____

_____

"Hate the sin, love the sinner."
Mahatma Gandhi

Day 307 – Is your physical health a mirror for your mental health? Why or why not?

_____

_____

_____

_____

_____

_____

_____

_____

_____

_____

Day 308 – Write down your own philosophy on life in five sentences maximum.

_____

_____

_____

_____

_____

_____

_____

_____

_____

_____

"A poem begins as a lump in the throat, a sense of wrong, a homesickness, a lovesickness."
Robert Frost

Day 309 - What past mistake are you still dwelling on?

Day 310 - When was the last time you lied to protect your image?

"It is the mark of an educated mind to be able to entertain a thought without accepting it."
Aristotle, *Metaphysics*

Day 311 - What made you smile today?

_____
_____
_____
_____
_____
_____
_____
_____
_____
_____

Day 312 - What is your biggest challenge when it comes to social anxiety?

_____
_____
_____
_____
_____
_____
_____
_____
_____
_____

"You may not control all the events that happen to you, but you can decide not to be reduced by them."
Maya Angelou, *Letter to My Daughter*

Day 313 - If you're being honest, is your happiness dependent on others? Why or why not?

_____

_____

_____

_____

_____

_____

_____

_____

_____

Day 314 - Do you often feel the need to apologize?

_____

_____

_____

_____

_____

_____

_____

_____

_____

**"You never know what worse luck
your bad luck has saved you from."**
Cormac McCarthy, *No Country for Old Men*

Day 315 - Write down your three best memories from last year.

_____

_____

_____

_____

_____

_____

_____

_____

_____

_____

Day 316 - What are three small actions you could take to
improve your patience?

_____

_____

_____

_____

_____

_____

_____

_____

_____

_____

"An expert is a person who has made all the mistakes
that can be made in a very narrow field."
Niels Bohr

Day 317 - If you keep the same job, how would your
professional life look like 5 years from now?

_____
_____
_____
_____
_____
_____
_____
_____
_____

Day 318 - What beauty have you created in the past
few months?

_____
_____
_____
_____
_____
_____
_____
_____
_____
_____

"You think your pain and your heartbreak are unprecedented in the history of the world, but then you read."
James Baldwin

Day 319 - What are the three first things you would tell a stranger about yourself.

Day 320 - What is your biggest challenge when it comes to forgiving?

"Education is the ability to listen to almost anything without losing your temper or your self-confidence."
Robert Frost

Day 321 - Is what you're doing today positively impacting your long-term future?

_____

_____

_____

_____

_____

_____

_____

_____

_____

Day 322 - Write down five material possessions you feel grateful for.

_____

_____

_____

_____

_____

_____

_____

_____

_____

_____

"Wise men speak because they have something to say; fools because they have to say something."
Plato

Day 323 - What make you feel thankful for the changes you've made in the past year?

_____

_____

_____

_____

_____

_____

_____

_____

Day 324 - What three questions would you ask a medical specialist?

_____

_____

_____

_____

_____

_____

_____

_____

**"I have decided to stick to love...
Hate is too great a burden to bear."**
Martin Luther King Jr., *A Testament of Hope*

Day 325 - How could you practice gratitude to other people?

Day 326 - What is your strategy for planning out a holiday?

"Sometimes when I'm talking, my words can't keep up with my thoughts. I wonder why we think faster than we speak. Probably so we can think twice."
Bill Watterson

Day 327 - How do you see your life three months for now?

Day 328 - Write down seven things in your home you could easily give or throw away.

"The one thing we can never get enough of is love.
And the one thing we never give enough of is love."
Henry Miller

Day 329 - What is your biggest challenge when it comes to self-acceptance?

_____

_____

_____

_____

_____

_____

_____

_____

_____

Day 330 - If you could have three wishes for the world, what would they be?

_____

_____

_____

_____

_____

_____

_____

_____

_____

"It's kind of fun to do the impossible."
Walt Disney

Day 331 - Write down a top 7 from your most important areas in life, such as health, family, love life and finances.

_____

_____

_____

_____

_____

_____

_____

_____

_____

Day 332 - What is your favorite strategy for dramatizing your own feelings?

_____

_____

_____

_____

_____

_____

_____

_____

_____

_____

"The best moments in reading are when you come across
something – a thought, a feeling, a way of looking at things –
which you had thought special and particular to you.
Now here it is, set down by someone else,
a person you have never met, someone even who is long dead.
And it is as if a hand has come out and taken yours."
Alan Bennett, *The History Boys*

Day 333 - What is life all about?

Day 334 - What is your favorite book and why?

**"Never stop smiling not even when you're sad,
someone might fall in love with your smile."**
Gabriel Garcia Marquez

Day 335 - What is the first step you need to take right now to achieve your ideal social life?

_____

_____

_____

_____

_____

_____

_____

_____

_____

Day 336 - What would your 15-year old self say about your life today?

_____

_____

_____

_____

_____

_____

_____

_____

_____

"Drop the idea of becoming someone, because you are already a masterpiece. You cannot be improved.
You have only to come to it, to know it, to realize it."
Osho

Day 337 - What would you like to avoid at all costs?

_____

_____

_____

_____

_____

_____

_____

_____

_____

Day 338 - What do you need in your life right now?

_____

_____

_____

_____

_____

_____

_____

_____

_____

*"To learn what we fear is to learn who we are.
Horror defies our boundaries and illuminates our souls."*
Shirley Jackson, *The Haunting of Hill House*

Day 339 - What would you do differently if you'd won 10 million dollars in a lottery today?

_____

_____

_____

_____

_____

_____

_____

_____

_____

_____

Day 340 - What thoughts consumed most of your time today?

_____

_____

_____

_____

_____

_____

_____

_____

_____

_____

**"Tell me then, does love make one a fool
or do only fools fall in love?"**
Orhan Pamuk, *My Name Is Red*

Day 341 - What do you really want out of a love relationship?

_____

_____

_____

_____

_____

_____

_____

_____

_____

_____

Day 342 - What did you love to do between the age of 7 and 14?

_____

_____

_____

_____

_____

_____

_____

_____

_____

_____

_____

"Respect was invented to cover the empty place where love should be."
Leo Tolstoy, *Anna Karenina*

Day 343 - What would you be happy to spend the next 20 year of your life doing?

Day 344 - Does your career fulfill you?

**"Life is a drama full of tragedy and comedy.
You should learn to enjoy the comic episodes a little more."**
Jeannette Walls, *The Glass Castle*

Day 345 - What is your favorite way to learn new things?

_____

_____

_____

_____

_____

_____

_____

_____

_____

_____

Day 346 - What do you really want out of a friendship?

_____

_____

_____

_____

_____

_____

_____

_____

_____

_____

_____

**"When you consider things like the stars,
our affairs don't seem to matter very much, do they?"**
Virginia Woolf

Day 347 - List down 5 reasons why you're doing the work
you do.

_____

_____

_____

_____

_____

_____

_____

_____

Day 348 - Reflect on the 5 reasons you wrote yesterday. How
does these reasons make you feel? Is it time for a change?

_____

_____

_____

_____

_____

_____

_____

_____

"We have the marvelous gift of making everything insignificant."
Nikolai Gogol

Day 349 - What does your strengths and skill set allow you to do?

_____

_____

_____

_____

_____

_____

_____

_____

_____

_____

Day 350 - What is the first step you need to take right now, to achieve your ideal financial situation?

_____

_____

_____

_____

_____

_____

_____

_____

_____

_____

"At some point in life the world's beauty becomes enough.
You don't need to photograph, paint, or even remember it.
It is enough."
Toni Morrison

Day 351 – Sit down for fifteen minutes without doing anything.
Set the alarm clock. Afterward, reflect back on it.
What happened?

_____

_____

_____

_____

_____

_____

_____

_____

_____

Day 352 – What is for you easier to learn than for others?

_____

_____

_____

_____

_____

_____

_____

_____

_____

"I don't know where I'm going, but I'm on my way."
Carl Sandburg

Day 353 – Sit down for fifteen minutes without doing anything.
Set the alarm clock. Afterwards reflect back on it.
What happened?

_____

_____

_____

_____

_____

_____

_____

_____

_____

Day 354 – What do you really want out of a job/career?

_____

_____

_____

_____

_____

_____

_____

_____

_____

"Beware, O wanderer, the road is walking too."
Jim Harrison, *After Ikkyu & Other Poems*

Day 355 – What things in life do you take for granted?

Day 356 – Do you feel you deserve to be happy?

"Who wishes to fight must first count the cost."
Sun Tzu, *The Art of War*

Day 357 – What life lessons would you give to a class of 15-year olds?

Day 358 – Where in your life do you need guidance? How could you find this guidance?

"If you can't fly then run, if you can't run then walk,
if you can't walk then crawl,
but whatever you do you have to keep moving forward."
Martin Luther King Jr.

Day 359 - If you could be with your 12-year old self for one day, what would you do? And what would you say?

Day 360 - Can you still find your inner child?

"Stupidity lies in wanting to draw conclusions."
Gustave Flaubert

Day 361 - Imagine you could clean up your mind, where would you begin?

_____

_____

_____

_____

_____

_____

_____

_____

_____

Day 362 - What are your thoughts on social media?

_____

_____

_____

_____

_____

_____

_____

_____

_____

_____

"Sometimes letting things go is an act of far greater power than defending or hanging on."
Eckhart Tolle, *A New Earth*

Day 363 – What one belief would you want to let go off?

_____

_____

_____

_____

_____

_____

_____

_____

_____

_____

Day 364 – What fantasies makes you feel alive and hopeful?

_____

_____

_____

_____

_____

_____

_____

_____

_____

_____

_____

"If a man does not keep pace with his companions, perhaps it is because he hears a different drummer. Let him step to the music which he hears, however measured or far away. "
Henry David Thoreau

Day 365 – Write a letter to your future self and open it one year from now.

Personal Journal

The Self-Exploration Journal

One Year. A New Question Every Day

CREATED BY:

Zen Mirrors

Gold Amsterdam

2019

53274524R00126

Made in the USA
Columbia, SC
12 March 2019